Dear Parent:
Your child's love of reading

Every child learns to read in a different way and at his or her own speed. Some go back and forth between reading levels and read favorite books again and again. Others read through each level in order. You can help your young reader improve and become more confident by encouraging his or her own interests and abilities. From books your child reads with you to the first books he or she reads alone, there are I Can Read Books for every stage of reading:

SHARED READING
Basic language, word repetition, and whimsical illustrations, ideal for sharing with your emergent reader

BEGINNING READING
Short sentences, familiar words, and simple concepts for children eager to read on their own

READING WITH HELP
Engaging stories, longer sentences, and language play for developing readers

READING ALONE
Complex plots, challenging vocabulary, and high-interest topics for the independent reader

ADVANCED READING
Short paragraphs, chapters, and exciting themes for the perfect bridge to chapter books

I Can Read Books have introduced children to the joy of reading since 1957. Featuring award-winning authors and illustrators and a fabulous cast of beloved characters, I Can Read Books set the standard for beginning readers.

A lifetime of discovery begins with the magical words "I Can Read!"

Visit www.icanread.com for information
on enriching your child's reading experience.

I Can Read Book® is a trademark of HarperCollins Publishers.

The Voyage of the *Dawn Treader*: Aboard the *Dawn Treader* Text copyright © 2010 by C.S. Lewis Pte. Ltd. Photographs copyright © 2010 by Twentieth Century Fox Film Corporation and Walden Media, LLC. All rights reserved. Printed in the United States of America. No part of this book may be used or reproduced in any manner whatsoever without written permission except in the case of brief quotations embodied in critical articles and reviews. For information address HarperCollins Children's Books, a division of HarperCollins Publishers, 10 East 53rd Street, New York, NY 10022.
www.icanread.com

Library of Congress catalog card number: 2010929546
ISBN 978-0-06-196909-6

Typography by Rick Farley

10 11 12 13 LP/WOR 10 9 8 7 6 5 4 3 2

First Edition

Aboard the Dawn Treader

Adapted by Jennifer Frantz

Based on the screenplay by
Christopher Markus & Steve McFeely
and Michael Petroni

Based on the book by C. S. Lewis

HARPER

An Imprint of HarperCollinsPublishers

WHOOSH!

A strong wind fills the sails

of a great wooden ship.

The *Dawn Treader*

is sailing off

on a big adventure!

The *Dawn Treader*

is the royal ship

of King Caspian X, ruler of Narnia.

A ship like no other,

the *Dawn Treader* is carved

from the finest wood.

She has a grand dragon head,

and the seal of the great Aslan.

Caspian is a fearless leader.

He is always ready

for any quest.

Now he is on a mission

to find the seven lost lords

of Narnia.

Lord Drinian is the captain
of the *Dawn Treader.*
He is a noble and
honest seaman.

At the wheel,

Lord Drinian makes

no mistakes.

He watches the sky and the sea.

He carefully steers

the *Dawn Treader* onward.

Lucy and Edmund Pevensie
have joined Caspian,
Lord Drinian and the crew
for this adventure.

At home in England,

Lucy and Edmund

are regular children.

But in Narnia,

Lucy and Edmund are royalty!

Lucy is Queen Lucy the Valiant.

And Edmund is King Edmund the Just.

Lucy and Edmund

have one small problem . . .

. . . their cousin Eustace

has tagged along.

Eustace is a coward

and a complainer.

Even worse, he doesn't believe

in Narnia or magic.

Eustace will have a lot to learn
aboard the *Dawn Treader*!

Sir Reepicheep, the bravest

and most noble mouse

in all of Narnia,

is also on board.

He is ready to serve—

no matter the danger!

Sir Reepicheep

is even teaching Eustace

a thing or two

about sword fighting!

Caspian helps Edmund brush up
on his sword fighting, too.

With a boat full of brave souls,

the *Dawn Treader* will go

to the end of the world

to find the seven lost lords of Narnia.

No one knows what

this daring voyage will bring.

But one thing is certain—

it will be an adventurous ride!